SHEEP SCHOOL

ROSS MONTGOMERY

ILLUSTRATED BY
MARISA MOREA

Barrington Stoke

First published in 2023 in Great Britain by
Barrington Stoke Ltd
18 Walker Street, Edinburgh, EH3 7LP

www.barringtonstoke.co.uk

Text © 2023 Ross Montgomery
Illustrations © 2023 Marisa Morea

A CIP catalogue record for this book is available
from the British Library upon request

ISBN: 978-1-80090-193-3

Printed by Hussar Books, Poland

This book is in a super-readable format for young readers
beginning their independent reading journey.

For Raife

CONTENTS

CHAPTER 1
WILLIAM

It was another day at Sheep School. All the lambs were working hard in their classrooms, sitting still and in perfect rows ...

Well, *almost* all the lambs.

"SIT DOWN, WILLIAM!" shouted Miss Bleater.

William wasn't working hard. He was tap-dancing on his chair and singing at the top of his lungs, as usual.

"Oh! Sorry, Miss Bleater," he said. "I don't know what came over me."

William sat down and the other lambs giggled.

Everyone knew William was the worst sheep in Sheep School.

The other lambs were all brilliant at doing things like sitting still, not talking, doing what the teacher said – all the things a sheep was meant to do. But William couldn't sit still for more than a few seconds before he burst into song and dance. He didn't mean to be bad – he just couldn't do anything else!

His teacher, Miss Bleater, gave him an angry look.

"As I was trying to say, before one of you was so rude," she said. "We have an important day coming up! Does everyone remember what we're all doing in Big Field tomorrow morning?"

"Standing still," replied all the lambs together.

William groaned.

Standing still was the most important skill a sheep could learn – and the one he was worst at by miles.

"That's right!" said Miss Bleater. "And tell me, class – *why* is standing still so important?"

"Because it protects us from the wolves," said the lambs.

Everyone shivered. All the sheep in William's flock were terrified of the wolves in the nearby woods.

Their leader, the Big Bad Wolf, kept coming up with clever new ways to steal sheep and carry them back to his den.

"Correct!" said Miss Bleater. "For years, sheep have been afraid of the Big Bad Wolf – but now we know that standing still is the only way to be safe in a wolf attack. At least, that's what our new headmaster tells us!"

She turned to look at the picture of the new headmaster. His name was Mr Howler and all the other lambs loved him.

William frowned. He always got
a funny feeling when he looked at
Mr Howler's picture.

There was something odd about
his toothy grin and pointy ears. And
William thought his fleece looked like
a bad wig.

"Mr Howler is the best headmaster that we've ever had!" said Miss Bleater. "Tomorrow is our chance to show him how good our standing-still skills are – and *no one* is going to mess it up."

She looked hard at William. "Isn't that right, William?"

The whole class turned to glare at William.

"You heard me!" said Miss Bleater. "No dancing! No singing! No home-made costumes!"

"I thought you liked my costumes," said William, pointing at his rainbow boots.

"Of course I don't!" snapped Miss Bleater. "Remember the most important rule of Sheep School: A LOYAL SHEEP PROTECTS THEIR FLOCK. And singing and dancing is no way to protect your fellow sheep from a wolf attack. It's time you stopped trying to stand out and learned how to fit in! Tomorrow is your last chance, William. If you mess up tomorrow, I will have to EXPEL you from Sheep School!"

All the other lambs gasped. No one had ever been thrown out of Sheep School before!

William gulped. If he was expelled from Sheep School, his parents would never forgive him. All they wanted was for him to be a perfect sheep. They were going to be in Big Field tomorrow too – Mr Howler had said that every sheep in the flock had to take part.

If William was the only sheep who couldn't stand still, his parents would be very upset!

Miss Bleater was right – tomorrow William *had* to stand still like everyone else. No matter what, he must not sing or act or dance or juggle. But how was he ever going to do that? He could only last a few seconds before he just had to burst into a song-and-dance routine!

Do it, William, he thought to himself. *For Mum and Dad. After all – how hard can it be to stand still for a few seconds?*

CHAPTER 2
THE BIG DAY

It was the next morning. The whole flock was in Big Field, waiting for the show to begin. William had never seen so many sheep in one place before. He felt sick with nerves.

"Remember," he whispered to himself. "Just stay still – it'll all be over soon ..."

"Places, everyone!" said Miss Bleater. "Mr Howler is here!"

All the lambs *baaah*ed as Mr Howler stood in front of them. Once again, William thought there was something odd about their new headmaster – maybe it was all the saliva dripping from his mouth.

"Good morning, my fellow sheep!"
Mr Howler said in a loud voice. He
sounded even more growly than usual.
"You're looking very delicious ... I mean,
er, healthy today!"

Mr Howler looked over at the
woods. William frowned – it looked like
Mr Howler was waiting for something.
But what?

"Now, don't forget," said Mr Howler.
"Standing still is the most important
skill a sheep can learn. If the Big Bad
Wolf and his wolf pack suddenly show

up, the only way to protect yourself is by closing your eyes and standing totally still. Let's all practise – the whole flock! Ten minutes of silence!"

William's mouth fell open. *Ten minutes?!* He'd never even stood still for ten seconds before! How was he going to do that?

He looked across Big Field ... and saw his mum and dad. Mum had worn her best hat. Dad was giving him a proud thumbs up.

William's heart sank. He couldn't let them down. He had to do this perfectly or he'd be expelled from Sheep School.

The other lambs stood in a perfect line, ready to begin. William got ready too.

"All right, everyone?" cried Mr Howler, looking back at the woods a second time. "3, 2, 1 … STAND STILL!"

Every sheep in the field closed their eyes and locked to the spot. No one made a sound.

William screwed his eyes shut – he had to get this right! His parents were counting on him.

Don't mess this up, William! It's your last chance ...

But he could already tell that it was no use. His hooves were itching to dance. His legs were beginning to

tremble. His woolly face needed a
scratch ...

*Come on – stay still! Just make sure
you don't think of any catchy tunes, like
dum-di-ditty-dum, DA DA DAH ...*

Too late. William leapt up like a firework, somersaulted in the air and ended up doing the splits in the middle of the field.

"TAAAA-BAAAAAAH!" he sang.

A hundred pairs of shocked sheepy eyes stared back at him. No one could believe what they had just seen.

"Er … what's going on?" said
Mr Howler, looking puzzled.

Miss Bleater shook with anger.

"WILLIAM! That was the last straw!"
She pointed at him. "You give me no
choice – you are *expelled* from Sheep
School!"

The entire flock gasped – William was too shocked to even reply.

He looked over at his parents. He had never seen them look so sad.

Mr Howler waved his hooves about.

"Er … never mind about him!" he snapped, looking over at the woods again. "Let's have another try, shall we? And don't forget, you must keep your eyes closed!"

William couldn't listen to any more. He saw his parents shake their heads and turn their backs on him. They didn't even want to look at him. He was the only sheep who couldn't stand still. He was the shame of the whole flock.

William left Big Field by himself and he didn't look back.

"Goodbye, Mum," he whispered as he began to cry. "Goodbye, Dad. Goodbye, everyone."

CHAPTER 3
SHEEP SHOCK!

William plodded up the hill, away from everything he had ever known. He had no idea where he was going to go or what he was going to do. But he knew that he didn't belong here.

He took one last look at his flock.
They were all standing still in Big Field
while Mr Howler watched over them,
grinning. William's heart sank. He had
tried his best to be just like them ... but
his best was never good enough.

"Maybe I was never meant to
be a sheep," said William sadly.
"Maybe I should be a pig or a duck
or something ..."

A very loud noise made him look up again. Some big trucks were driving out of the woods and speeding towards Big Field – and the trucks were being driven by wolves! The sheep in his flock couldn't see – they all had their eyes shut.

"It's a wolf attack!" William gasped. "Someone has to stop them!"

But who?

The wolves leapt out of the trucks and ran into Big Field, licking their lips. They picked up the sheep two at a time and threw them into the trucks as if they were picking apples.

The sheep knew what was happening, but they didn't run away. They stayed stock-still with their eyes closed. That was what Mr Howler had told them to do in a wolf attack. But it didn't stop the wolves one bit.

"Standing still doesn't work at all!" cried William. "Why isn't Mr Howler doing something?"

William looked at Mr Howler – and gasped. The headmaster had taken off his fleece ... and underneath was a coat of thick fur.

William had been right – his sheepy fleece *was* a wig after all! Mr Howler gave a big, mean smile, showing a row of razor-sharp teeth.

Mr Howler was no sheep – he was the Big Bad Wolf himself!

"Good job, wolves!" he growled. "I *knew* my plan would work. These sheep are even more stupid than they look!"

He jumped onto the nearest truck. "Quick! Time to take them back to my den and have a sheep feast!"

The wolves cheered and then sped into the woods with all the sheep. William could hear the frantic *baaaahs* as the trucks vanished into the trees.

"It was all a trick!" said William. "I have to do something. If I don't, my whole flock will get gobbled up ... AND my parents! But what can I do?"

William was just one lamb against the Big Bad Wolf and his whole gang. How could he do anything to help? After all, he was the worst sheep in Sheep School.

William gritted his teeth. *No!* He might have been expelled from Sheep School, but he was still a sheep. And just like Miss Bleater said, a loyal sheep *always* protects their flock.

He looked at the woods where the trucks had gone.

"I can follow the tyre tracks to find the Big Bad Wolf's den," he said to himself. "But what do I do then? I can't fight one wolf, let alone ten. I don't have any skills!"

William stopped – he *did* have skills. There was no sheep anywhere that was better at singing and dancing and acting and making costumes than him.

He spotted a farmer's cottage on the hill beside him. William could see a wardrobe through the window.

"Time to save the day," he grinned. "And this time, I'm going to do it *my* way!"

CHAPTER 4
THE BIG BAD WOLF

William peered through the bushes. In the middle of the forest stood a wooden fortress with a tall, spiked fence, guarded by two mean-looking wolves. As William watched, the doors opened and the Big Bad Wolf walked out with the rest of his gang.

"We're off to collect some wood so we can roast these sheep!" the Big Bad Wolf barked at the guards. "You two stay here and make sure no one escapes!"

William gasped. He could see his flock in the middle of the fortress, trapped in a huge wooden cage. He could see the other lambs, and Miss Bleater, and his mum and dad. They all looked so frightened. He had to save them!

William saw the two guards stand up straight and salute the Big Bad Wolf as he and his gang walked off.

He gulped – how could he get past the guards and break out a hundred sheep?

William took a deep breath and stepped out of the bushes. He had made himself a brilliant costume – his best one yet.

He'd tied three old fur coats around himself to look like wolf's fur and made himself a long snout from an old stale baguette. He started to whistle a happy tune and strode up to the guards.

"Halt!" cried one of the guards. "Who goes there?"

William was scared ... but he was a very good actor.

"Who am I?" he growled, and he sounded just like a wolf. "Why, I'm the chef that's come to roast the sheep! The Big Bad Wolf asked me to come and cook a delicious meal for you all. Let me inside at once."

The wolf guards looked at each other, puzzled.

"The Big Bad Wolf didn't say anything about a chef," said one. "Shall we wait until he comes back and check with him first ...?"

"No!" said William quickly. "It's ... a surprise! To thank you for all your hard work today. He wants this feast to be extra special. That's why you'll be getting *double portions*!"

The guards licked their lips.

"Double portions?" said one.

"Get inside quick!" the other one whispered. "And start cooking. I'm starving!"

William walked through the gates –
then, quick as flash, he slammed them
shut and locked them. The guards yelled
and pounded at the doors, but it was no
use – they were trapped outside!

William knew he didn't have long.
The guards would bring the other wolves
back in no time.

He pulled off his fake wolf fur and fake snout and ran to the sheep cage. His flock couldn't believe it was him.

"W-William?" cried Miss Bleater. "What are you doing here?"

"Helping you escape, that's what!" said William. "A loyal sheep always protects his flock, remember?"

"But you won't get us out in time!" said Dad. "This cage is locked, and the Big Bad Wolf has the only key."

William looked at the giant padlock on the cage door. Dad was right – he'd never be able to pick the lock.

"Run, William!" said Mum. "Leave while you still can!"

But William had an idea. "Stand back, everybody!" he cried.

The sheep *baaahed* and stepped back.

William took a deep breath ... and then ran towards the cage. He did a perfect somersault, then swung his leg towards the wooden cage bars and ... *SNAP!* He split three of them in two, leaving a hole big enough for the sheep to escape.

"Quick! Everyone out!" said William. "We don't have much time before those guards catch up with the Big Bad Wolf and—"

"STOP – RIGHT – THERE!"

William was already too late. The fortress doors were broken open – and there, standing at the gates with his gang, was the Big Bad Wolf, grinning from ear to ear!

CHAPTER 5
THE FINAL FIGHT

"Well, well, well!" said the Big Bad Wolf. "Looks like there's an *extra* sheep for us to eat at the feast tonight!" He pointed a razor-sharp claw at William. "Guards – grab him!"

The wolves started creeping forwards, licking their lips.

The sheep trembled and tried to hide – but William stood still.

"We can't give up now!" he said.
"There's only ten wolves and a hundred
of us. We have to fight back!"

"But how?" said Miss Bleater. "There's
no way a sheep can ever win a fight
against a wolf!"

"So?" said William. "We might not be able to fight, but we all have skills we can use!"

"Like what?" asked the lambs all together.

William's brain whirred ... and came up with a brilliant idea.

"Sheep are great at doing what they're told – so do this!" he shouted. "Everyone – stand in a line!"

The sheep did what they were told right away. In two seconds, all one hundred sheep stood in two perfect rows in front of the wolves.

"Now, everyone – charge!" William cried.

The sheep raced forwards like a great woolly wall. The wolves tried to fight back, but they were no match against a hundred sheep working together.

Soon every wolf had been trampled into the ground. Even the Big Bad Wolf was knocked over by the charging sheep!

"Come on, lads – fight back!" he snapped at his wolf gang.

"Oh no you don't!" shouted William. He made sure every sheep could hear him. "NOW FOR THE MOST IMPORTANT SKILL OF ALL … EVERYONE, STAND STILL!"

All one hundred sheep stood on top of the wolves – and locked in place.

There was nothing the wolves could do. They kicked and cursed, but they were pinned to the ground by ten sheep each.

"We did it!" cried the sheep. "We beat the Big Bad Wolf!"

"Three cheers for William!" chanted the lambs.

Everyone cheered. William couldn't believe it. The flock all loved him now. His parents looked very proud and happy. Miss Bleater clapped a hoof on his back.

"I was wrong about you, William," she said. "I should never have expelled you from Sheep School – you're the most loyal sheep of all! How can I ever repay you?"

William grinned.

"Well ... I guess that we'll need a new headmaster now that Mr Howler's gone," he said. "I've got a few ideas of what we can do ..."

*

Big Field was full of action. Sheep for miles around were doing cartwheels, twirling ribbons and tap-dancing. Mum and Dad were practising their stand-up comedy routine. Even Miss Bleater was busting out her best disco moves!

"That's it!" William shouted. "Great job, everyone! This talent show is going to be the best one yet!"

Sheep School was now the *William Academy of Performing BaaaaaArts* – and it was totally different. Instead of learning how to stand still, the new headmaster was teaching the sheep everything he knew about singing and dancing!

All the sheep had their own special skills.

Some were making posters, some were playing music, and some were helping set up the lights for the show.

William had helped them understand something important: you don't need to be like everyone else in order to fit in.

William smiled. He had always felt like the outsider of his flock – but now, at last, he belonged.

TAH-BAAAAAAH!